To everybody at Boxer Books
J.A.

First American edition published in 2010
by Boxer Books Limited.

Distributed in the United States and Canada by
Sterling Publishing Co., Inc.
387 Park Avenue South, New York, NY 10016-8810

First published in Great Britain in 2010
by Boxer Books Limited.
www.boxerbooks.com

Text and illustrations copyright © 2010 Jonathan Allen

The rights of Jonathan Allen to be identified as the author and
illustrator of this work have been asserted by him
in accordance with the Copyright, Designs and Patents Act, 1988.

The illustrations were hand drawn and colored in Corel Painter IX using a Wacom tablet and pen.
The text is set in ITC Garamond Book.

ISBN 978-1-907152-54-2

1 3 5 7 9 10 8 6 4 2

Printed in China

All of our papers are sourced from managed forests and renewable resources.

WHEN THE SNOW COMES

JONATHAN ALLEN

BOXER BOOKS

In a meadow, high up in the mountains,

Little Yak was looking at the sky.

Big, gray clouds were gathering.

"The snow is coming, Little Yak,"
said Mom.

"Oh!" said Little Yak.

"I've never seen snow before."

Little Yak ran down to the stream
to tell his friend Pika.

"The snow is coming, Pika!"

said Little Yak.

"I know," said Pika.

"That's why I have been gathering grass, to feed me through the cold winter."

"Oh," said Little Yak.

"Do yaks gather lots of grass to eat in the winter?"

"I don't know, Little Yak," said Pika.

"But I don't think so."

Then Little Yak saw his friend Blue
Thrush and ran up to him.

"Guess what, Blue Thrush," said Little Yak.

"The snow is coming!"

"You're right, Little Yak,"
said Blue Thrush.

"That's why my friends and I are flying off to our warm winter home."

"Oh," said Little Yak.

"Do yaks have a warm winter

home to go to?"

"I don't know, Little Yak,"

said Blue Thrush. "But I don't think so."

Little Yak's friend Brown Bear
came lumbering by.
Little Yak bounced up to him.
"Hello, Brown Bear,"
said Little Yak.
"Do you know
the snow is coming?"

"I do, Little Yak," said Brown Bear.

"That's why I have been
eating and eating all summer,
to put on enough fat to last
me through my
long winter sleep."

"Oh," said Little Yak.

"Do yaks have a long
winter sleep?"

"I don't know, Little Yak,"
said Brown Bear,
"but I don't think so."

Little Yak ran back to his mom.

"Mom?" said Little Yak. "When the snow comes, do yaks gather lots of grass to feed them through the winter, like Pika?"

"No, Little Yak," said Mom.

"Do yaks go away to their warm winter home like Blue Thrush?" asked Little Yak. "And do they put on lots of fat to last through their long winter sleep, like Brown Bear?"

"No, Little Yak," said Mom.

"Well, what *do* yaks do when the snow comes?" asked Little Yak. "We stay right where we are," said Mom. "Our thick shaggy coats keep us warm. And *little* yaks snuggle up close to their moms."

"Look, Mom, it's *really* snowing now!"
cried Little Yak.
"Well, you know what to do,"
said Mom.

Little Yak snuggled up close
to his mom. And the snow
fell all around them.

"Yaks are lucky when the snow
comes," Little Yak said to his mom
as they watched the snow gently falling.
"Why are we lucky, Little Yak?" asked Mom.

"While all the other animals are sleeping,
or hiding, or have gone away,"
said Little Yak, "yaks get to see the
beautiful snow!"